All for the Kids:
Yoga for Children

Yoga manual for teachers, parents, and caregivers.

Written by Nichole F. Rich, Ph.D.
Illustrated by Lisa Furness

All for the Kids: Yoga for Children
Copyright ©2017 Nichole F. Rich
Illustration Copyright © 2014 by Lisa Furness

ISBN 978-1506-902-83-5 PRINT

LCCN 2017901011

January 2017

Published and Distributed by
First Edition Design Publishing, Inc.
P.O. Box 20217, Sarasota, FL 34276-3217
www.firsteditiondesignpublishing.com

ALL RIGHTS RESERVED. No part of this book publication may be reproduced, stored in a retrieval system, or transmitted in any form or by any means — electronic, mechanical, photo-copy, recording, or any other — except brief quotation in reviews, without the prior permission of the author or publisher.

Although the author has have made every effort to ensure that the information in this book was correct at press time, the author does not assume and hereby disclaim any liability to any party for any loss, damage, or disruption caused by errors or omissions, whether such errors or omissions result from negligence, accident, or any other cause.

Dedicated to Alec IV and Bella

Introduction

If you have young children or have worked with young children you can appreciate their inquisitive minds, their curious questions, and their busy bodies. Children are fascinating and their energy can make us smile. However, there are those times that we need children to be still, to focus, and to listen in order to grow and learn. Everyone would agree that physical activity is important for children to release their energy. Did you know that it also contributes to brain growth and development? What if you heard that physical activity can actually be used to help calm children and allow them to slow their bodies down?

It is important to help teach children how to regulate their emotions and we need to ensure that they are being exposed to high quality experiences that will enable them to grow and develop. As they move through their early years they learn how to navigate through relationships, sustain attention, and adhere to rules. Depending on the nature of the child these tasks can be overwhelming or frustrating resulting in tantrums, increased energy, or even anxiety.

The National Research Council Institute of Medicine (2008) explains that any new experiences trigger brain growth and refine existing structures. Children begin to learn tasks and skills that build the foundation for everything else they will learn in life: basic counting, the alphabet, sharing, joint attention and communication. During this time, their brains are growing at a rapid pace. Physical activity can help take this one step further.

Finding the right physical activity that is consistent with developmental gross motor and cognitive skills is essential. In addition to seeking out dance lessons, gymnastics or team sports, parents are encouraged to locate yoga or martial arts classes for children. Both activities not only provide the opportunity to work on basic skills but takes it one step further to teach functional breathing, which can positively affect the nervous system to alleviate sensory overload. Balance, coordination, strength, and stability are all elements that are typical in these types of classes.

Welcome to All for the Kids Yoga Program

The instructions and information provided in this manual has been designed to enable any teacher, parent, or caregiver to successfully implement yoga with young children. Many times in my years as a teacher parents would ask me how I was easily able to keep a group of 15 preschool students focused. I have also heard many parents and teachers say, "But I don't know how to teach yoga". With that in mind I set out to create a program that would be simple to follow.

Breath

Through yoga children begin to learn how to utilize breath. The controlled focused breathing in these activities enables them to slow down their thoughts, manage emotions, and develop overall well-being. Included in this manual are instructions on walking children through utilizing breath. You can use it in isolation or before any sequence.

Postures and Sequences

As you look through the manual you will notice that poses are illustrated on a single page followed by the instructions. You may wish to photocopy the pictures on to heavy duty paper with the instructions on the reverse to make it easy to use during a group time. Simply hold up the picture to provide children with the visual. Read the instructions on the back of the card as they move their bodies into position. Each pose can be held for 10 breaths.

The manual also includes recommended sequences that you can follow. These are located in the section following the individual poses with instructions. You will notice that the sequences are set up so that the movements can flow into one another. Follow along with the sequences or create your own sequence.

**You will notice some of the postures include both and left and right side. When you follow the sequences make sure you have the children do both sides. You can either have them do right and left in succession or you can do one side, downward dog, and then the other side for standing postures.

Preparation

In a typical yoga class you will notice that ambience plays a role in creating an atmosphere that is calming. You may decide to select calming, instrumental music and dim lighting for yoga sessions with your child. If you do not have access to music or the ability to dim lights speaking in a calm, even tone will be just as helpful.

Use of a yoga mat or carpeted area is necessary to ensure safety as children move through the movements.

Beginning the Session

It is important to keep in mind that all children will learn differently. Some may rely on the visuals while others do better with verbal cues. Most children benefit from having both of the visuals and the verbal cues. In almost all cases it will be helpful if you also demonstrate the movements as you are providing instructions. In my instruction with children I have found that the majority are able to move into the posture easily when looking at the picture. If you would like to slow the children down and have them wait for each instruction it will be important to gain their attention first. You will find a script below that I find helpful in prefacing yoga instructions for students.

Script for beginning:
Today we are going to do some yoga. I need you all to put your listening ears on and keep your eyes on me.

While the instructions in the manual are written in a format to assist you in the language you might find that you adjust the language or words you use according to the children you are working with. Keep the session as natural as possible and feel free to add in your own cues that you think are helpful.

Be patient if you are just beginning this for the first time. You can start with just one or five postures as you start to become more comfortable in sharing yoga with your children.

Now you are ready to begin. I hope you find this manual helpful in helping your child or students achieve balance, better attention, and more calmness.

Namaste,

Nichole

Instructions for Breath Techniques

Balloon Breath

1. Lay on your back with both hands on your belly.
2. Pretend that your belly is a balloon. You need to fill the balloon with air.
3. Take a big breath and fill up the balloon.
4. Now let all the air out of the balloon. Make sure you get all of the air out. *Have them do this 3-5 times making sure that their bellies are rising each time.*
5. Practice this breath 5-10 times prior to at the end of yoga instruction.

Blowing Out Candles

1. Sit on your knees or lay on your back with one hand in front of your face and one hand on your belly.
2. Take a big breath in and feel your belly rise up.
3. Now pretend you are blowing out candles on a cake. Blow <u>all of the air out and feel the air on your hand.</u>
4. Practice this breath 5-10 times prior to at the end of yoga instruction.

Fog the Mirror
1. Sit on your knees or lay on your back with one hand in front of your face and one hand on your belly. (*You can have them use a real mirror to practice*)
2. Take a big breath in and feel your belly rise up.
3. Now pretend your hand is a mirror. Blow all of the air out of your belly and pretend you are fogging up the mirror.
4. Practice this breath 5-10 times prior to at the end of yoga instruction.

As the children begin to learn how to use their breath you may find that they will breathe in or out quickly. For young children, you will want to first model the breath and then have them do it together with you. Eventually, you will be able to count 2 seconds as they inhale and 2 seconds as they exhale while the children practice controlled breathing.

Airplane

Airplane

1. Stand tall on your mat.

2. Push your feet down into the mat and feel strong.

3. Slowly pick up your right leg behind you.
(You will do the same for the right side)

4. Tip your body forward.

5. Spread your arms out to the side or straight in front of you like an airplane.

Arrow

Arrow

1. Stand on your knees.

2. Keep your back up straight and tall.

3. Put your arms out to the side like an airplane.

3. Tip your body over to the side.

4. Put your left hand on the mat.
(*You will do the same for the right side*).

4. Make both of your legs straight.

5. Keep your left leg straight and move your right foot in front of you.

6. Bend the knee and hold yourself strong.

Boat

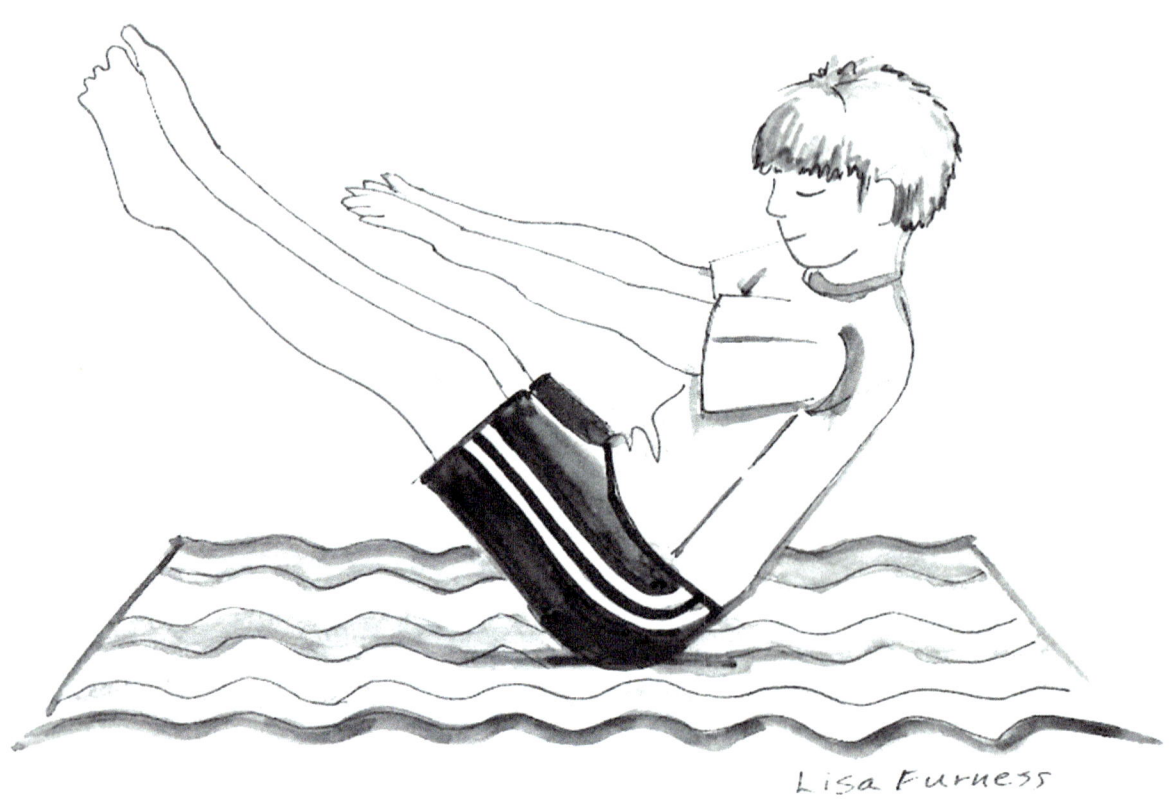

Boat

1. Sit tall on your mat. Keep your back up straight.

2. Put your hands on the mat behind you.

3. Press your legs together like they are glued.

4. Lift your legs up in front of you. Keep your knees bent if you need to balance.

5. Stretch your arms out in front of you to reach for your toes.

Bound Angle

Bound Angle

1. Sit up nice and tall.

2. Bring the bottom of your feet together.

3. Make your legs look like butterfly wings.

3. Wrap your hands around your toes.

4. Close your eyes and breathe.

Bridge

Bridge

1. Lay down on your back with your arms beside you.

2. Bend your knees and place your feet flat on the mat.

3. Push your feet into the mat and slowly lift your belly up to the sky.

Cat and Cow

Cat and Cow

1. Start on your hands and knees.

2. Put your hands under your shoulders.

3. Put your knees under your hips.

4. Breathe in and look up.

5. Pull your hips up to the sky.
(I have found it helpful to tell them to pretend they are a cat and lift their tails up to the sky).

6. Breathe out and bring your head down to look at your belly.

7. Pull your belly button up to the sky to round your back.

Chair

Chair

1. Stand tall on your mat and push your feet down into the mat.

2. Push your legs together and bend your knees.

3. Pretend you are sitting in a chair.

4. Reach your arms up to the sky.

Child's Pose

Child's Pose

1. Sit on your knees.

2. Keep your back up straight and tall.

3. Breathe in and slowly lower your body over your legs.

4. Bring your forehead all the way to the mat.

5. Put your arms behind you on the floor and breathe.

Cobra

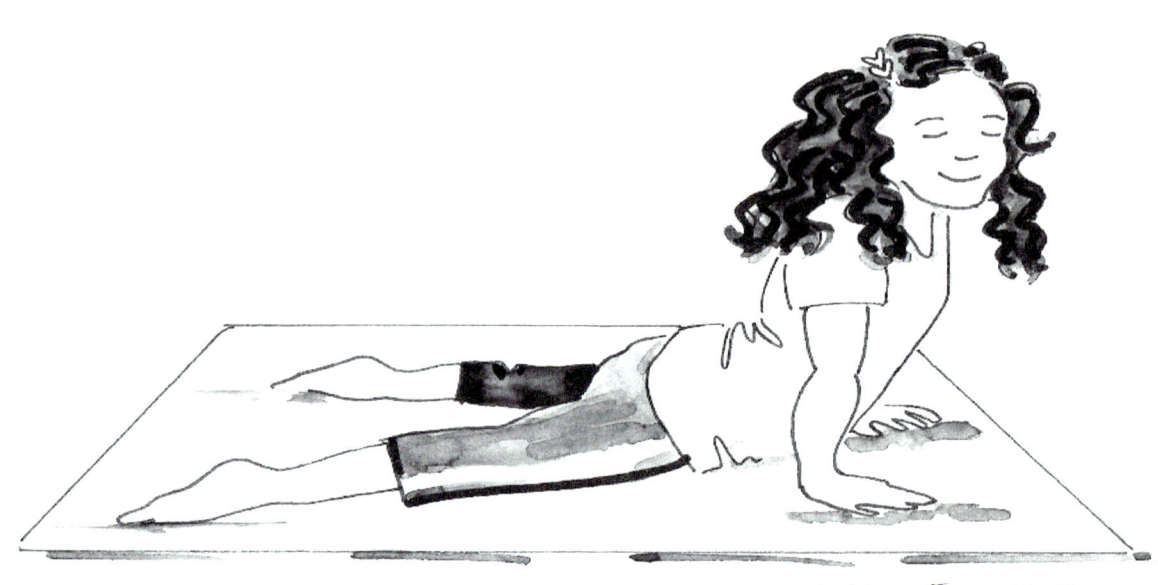

Cobra

1. Lie down on your belly and put your forehead on your hands.

2. Put your hands under your shoulders.

3. Spread your fingers wide and push your hands into the mat.

4. Keep your legs straight and strong. Reach your toes for the wall behind you.

5. Push your body up to make your arms straight and look up to the sky.

Dancer

Dancer

1. Stand tall on your mat. Push your feet into the mat.

2. Bend your right knee and bring your foot up behind you. (*You will do the same for the left leg*).

3. Reach your right hand back to hold onto your right ankle.

4. Stretch your left arm up high to the sky.

5. Bend forward and press your ankle into your hand.

Dolphin

Dolphin

1. Begin on your hands and knees.

2. Make a triangle on the mat with your arms. Hold your hands together to make the top of the triangle.

3. Push up to your toes and make your legs straight.

4. Tiptoe your feet toward your elbows.

Downward Dog

Downward Dog

1. Start on your hands and knees.

2. Curl your toes under and push up as you stretch your body to make a bridge.

3. Keep your legs straight and push your hips back.

4. Try and make your whole foot touch the floor.

5. Stay here and look at your knees.
(This will help them to drop their heads through their arms to get a full stretch through the shoulders.)

Dragon

Dragon

1. Stand on your knees. Keep your upper body up tall.

2. Put your right foot flat on the mat in front of you.
(You will do the same for the left foot.)

3. Raise your hands up to the sky.

4. Push your hips forward.

Forward Folding Bend

Forward Folding Bend

1. Sit down with your back up straight and your feet straight out in front.

2. Pretend your legs are glued together.

3. Raise your hands high up in the air and breathe in.

4. Breathe out and fold over your straight legs

5. Reach your hands for your toes.

6. Try and touch your nose to your knees.

Knee Hug

Knee Hug

1. Slowly lay down on your back.

2. Put your feet straight out in front of you.

3. Bring your knees in to your belly and wrap your arms around your knees.

4. Hug your knees gently.

Lying Twist

Lying Twist

1. Lay down on your mat and stretch your body long.

2. Bend your knees and put your feet flat on the floor.

3. Give yourself a knee hug. Glue your knees together.

4. Stretch your arms out to the side.

5. Keep your knees bent and lower your knees to the left.

6. Turn your head to the right.
(Repeat for the other side.)

Mountain

Mountain

1. Stand up nice and tall.

2. Pretend a string is pulling you up from the top of your head.

3. Keep your back up straight.

4. Keep your feet flat on the mat.

5. Put your hands by your side.

Lisa Furness

Plank

Plank

1. Lay down on your belly.

2. Put your hands under your shoulders.

3. Curl your toes under.

4. Push your body up and keep it straight.

Shark

Shark

1. Lie on your belly. Put your forehead on your hands.

2. Reach your toes for the wall behind you.

3. When you are ready, bring your hands behind your back and hold them together.

4. Roll your shoulders back and lift your head off the mat.

5. Pull your hands up behind you and slowly lift your legs off of the mat.

Lisa Furness

Spinal Twist

Spinal Twist

1. Sit up nice and tall with your legs straight out in front of you.

2. Point to your left foot.

3. Pick up your left foot and bend your knee.

4. Bring your foot over your right knee and put it flat on the floor.
(Some children can stop here and hold the knee while sitting up tall. You will do the same for the other side)

4. Wrap your right foot around to the left side of your body.

5. If you can, try and put your hand on the mat next to your foot.

6. Wrap your right elbow onto your left knee.

7. Place your left hand on the mat behind you.

Thunderbolt

Lisa Furness

Thunderbolt

1. Sit on your knees.

2. Keep your back up straight.

3. Focus your eyes forward.

Tree

Tree

1. Stand nice and tall. Feel strong in your body and push your feet into the mat.

2. Slowly raise your right foot and put it on the inside of your left ankle.
Make your toes touch the ground. Keep your heel on your ankle.
(This is called "sapling" and some children can stay here depending on balance)

3. When you feel strong, bring your foot up to the side of your knee.

4. When you feel balanced, bring your hands up to the sky like branches on a tree.

Triangle

Triangle

1. Stand up tall.

2. Put your right leg in front of you and point your toes forward.

3. Bring your left leg behind you. Turn your left foot out (or to the wall).

4. Turn your belly to the side.

3. Stretch your arms out like the letter "t".

4. Tip yourself over and bring your right hand to your right knee.
(Do the same for the left side)

5. Try and put your hand on the mat next to your foot.

6. Point your left hand to the sky. Keep your arm straight.

Warrior I

Warrior I

1. Stand on your mat.

2. Put your right foot in front.

3. Make sure your knee is over your ankle.
(*You will do the same for the left leg*)

4. Keep your back leg straight. (*The back toes will turn slightly out to a 45 degree angle*).

5. Slowly bring your upper body towards the sky.

6. Push your front foot and your back foot down into the mat. Pretend you are trying to push the mat away with your feet.

7. Raise your hands up to the sky.

Warrior II

Warrior II

1. Stand up tall.

2. Put your left leg in front of you and point your toes forward.

3. Bring your right leg behind you. Turn your right foot out (or to the wall).

4. Turn your belly to the side.

5. Stretch your arms out like the letter "t" or airplane wings.

Sequences I and II

Sequence I	Sequence II
Thunderbolt	Mountain
Knee Hug	Plank
Lying Twist	Downward Dog
Dragon	Plank
Plank	Downward Dog
Cobra	Warrior I
Downward Dog	Warrior II
Bound Angle	Triangle
Forward Folding Bend	Airplane
Spinal Twist	Tree
Child's Pose	Mountain

Sequences III and IV

Sequence III	Sequence IV
Mountain	Thunderbolt
Warrior I	Forward Folding Bend
Warrior II	Spinal Twist
Triangle	Forward Folding Bend
Downward Dog	Boat
Plank	Bridge
Cobra	Shark
Plank	Plank
Downward Dog	Downward Dog
Mountain	Dragon
	Mountain

Balance Sequence

Mountain
Chair
Tree
Airplane
Dancer
Mountain

Full Sequence

Mountain
Chair
Warrior I
Warrior II
Triangle
Downward Dog
Plank
Cobra
Shark
Plank
Downward Dog
Dragon
Arrow
Forward Folding Bend
Spinal Twist
Boat
Bridge
Dolphin
Plank
Tree
Airplane
Dancer
Knee Hug
Lying Twist
Child's Pose

About the Author

Nichole F. Rich, Ph.D., E-RYT200, is the founder and owner of Breathing Room Yoga and Wellness. She holds a 4th Degree Black Belt in Tae Kwon Do and has been studying martial arts since 1997. Dr. Rich began working with special needs students in 1999 as a teacher in the public school setting, working with children of all ages. She is a former elementary school principal and integrated preschool teacher. During her time training for her yoga certification she began using yoga as a tool to help her preschool students focus during instruction. She has trained teachers in public and private settings on integrating simple techniques to incorporate strategies for young children and traveled around the country in 2014 providing workshops for teachers on integrating yoga and movement in the classroom. She completed her doctoral research on yoga to increase attention in preschool students in 2010. Dr. Rich has presented her research as a guest speaker for Greenchools, Stonehill College, Wheaton College, The Discover You Expo and the Boston Association for the Education of Young Children. After becoming certified as a yoga teacher, she opened Breathing Room Yoga and Wellness, and became the founder of Yogarate, a fitness class for adults.. She received her BS in Early Childhood Education, M.Ed. in Special Education, CAGS in Educational Leadership all from Bridgewater State University and her Ph.D. in Curriculum and Instruction from Capella University. Dr. Rich lives in Norton, MA where she enjoys spending time training her two German Shepherds, Prana and Blaze.

About the Illustrator

Lisa Furness is a graduate of Rhode Island School of Design and has been involved in many creative projects over the years. While working with children in the public school setting, she realized that empowering children with tools to help them with their challenges is an issue she has a great passion for. She is pursuing a career as an author and illustrator writing stories for children about their emotional and social struggles and how they discover their own strengths that allow them to overcome their difficulties. Lisa resides in Massachusetts with her husband and 3 sons.